Why does a ball bounce?

Written by Sally Morgan

Illustrated by Barry Ablett

Collins

What's in this book?

Listen and say

football

basketball player

basketball

Download the audio at www.collins.co.uk/839709

tennis

bounce

table tennis

Mummy says, "Look at that basketball player. He's bouncing the ball."

We play many sports with lots of balls.

football

tennis

table tennis

Can you play these sports?

cricket

golf

basketball

Can you find some balls in
your house?
Count the balls you have got.

Is there a big ball? Is there a small ball? Do all the balls bounce?

9

This is a rubber band.

You can make a rubber band long and short.

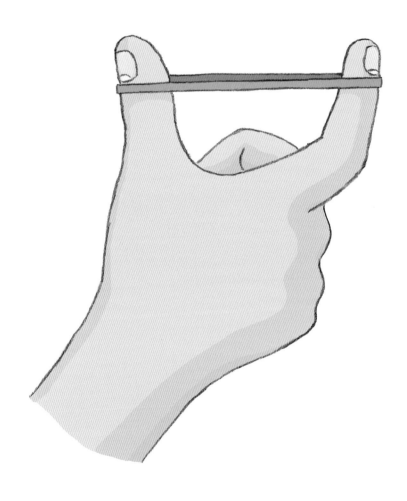

This is a rubber band ball. It bounces. Can you make a rubber band ball and bounce it?

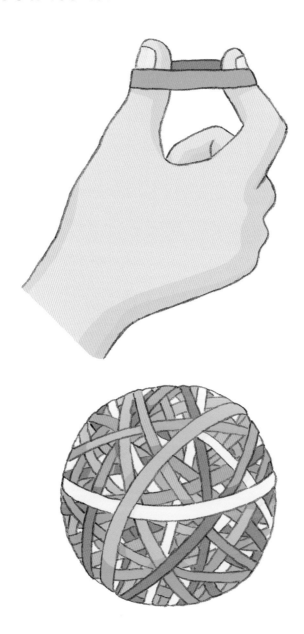

Hold a small rubber ball in your hand.
Press the ball.

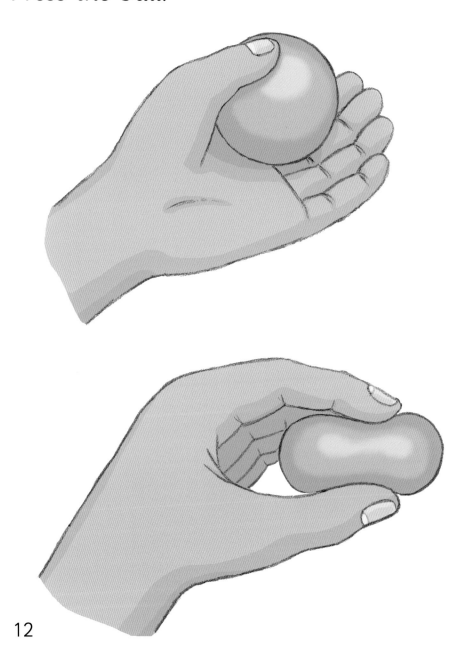

Now don't press. The ball is round again.

Why? The ball is rubber.
Rubber bounces.

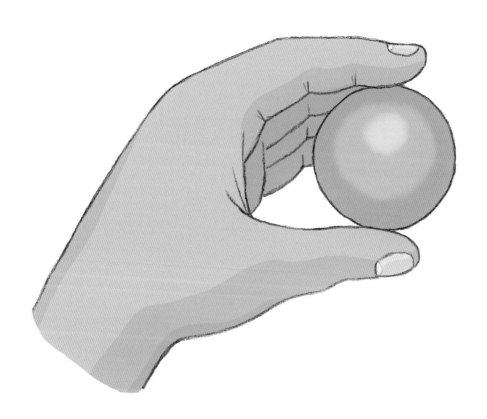

Drop a ball on the floor.

It bounces. Count the bounces.

Have you got a ball with a *big* bounce?

Find some tennis balls and a box.
Put the box on the floor.

Can you bounce the tennis balls into the box?

Bounce the ball in your garden.

Bounce the ball at the park.

Bounce the ball in your home.
Where is good to play?

Play a game!

Bounce the ball with one hand and count. Can you bounce the ball ten times?

Picture dictionary

Listen and repeat

ball

bounce

drop

press

rubber

rubber band

1 Look and match

basketball   **tennis ball**

football   **golf ball**

2 Listen and say

Download a reading guide for parents and teachers at
www.collins.co.uk/839709

Collins

Published by Collins
An imprint of HarperCollins*Publishers*
Westerhill Road
Bishopbriggs
Glasgow
G64 2QT

HarperCollins*Publishers*
1st Floor, Watermarque Building
Ringsend Road
Dublin 4
Ireland

William Collins' dream of knowledge for all began with the publication of his first book in 1819.

A self-educated mill worker, he not only enriched millions of lives, but also founded a flourishing publishing house. Today, staying true to this spirit, Collins books are packed with inspiration, innovation and practical expertise. They place you at the centre of a world of possibility and give you exactly what you need to explore it.

© HarperCollins*Publishers* Limited 2020

10 9 8 7 6 5 4 3 2

ISBN 978-0-00-839709-8

Collins® and COBUILD® are registered trademarks of HarperCollins*Publishers* Limited

www.collins.co.uk/elt

All rights reserved. No part of this publication may be reproduced, stored in a retrieval system, or transmitted in any form by any means, electronic, mechanical, photocopying, recording or otherwise, without the prior written permission of the Publisher or a licence permitting restricted copying in the United Kingdom issued by the Copyright Licensing Agency Ltd, 5th Floor, Shackleton House, 4 Battle Bridge Lane, London SE1 2HX.

British Library Cataloguing in Publication Data

A catalogue record for this publication is available from the British Library.

All rights reserved. No part of this book may be reproduced, stored in a retrieval system, or transmitted in any form or by any means, electronic, mechanical, photocopying, recording or otherwise, without the prior permission in writing of the Publisher. This book is sold subject to the conditions that it shall not, by way of trade or otherwise, be lent, re-sold, hired out or otherwise circulated without the Publisher's prior consent in any form of binding or cover other than that in which it is published and without a similar condition including this condition being imposed on the subsequent purchaser.

Author: Sally Morgan
Illustrator: Barry Ablett (Beehive)
Series editor: Rebecca Adlard
Commissioning editor: Zoë Clarke
Publishing manager: Lisa Todd
Product managers: Jennifer Hall and Caroline Green
In-house editor: Alma Puts Keren
Project manager: Emily Hooton
Editor: Barbara MacKay
Proofreaders: Natalie Murray and Michael Lamb
Cover designer: Kevin Robbins
Typesetter: 2Hoots Publishing Services Ltd
Audio produced by id audio, London
Reading guide author: Emma Wilkinson
Production controller: Rachel Weaver
Printed and bound by: GPS Group, Slovenia

MIX
Paper from
responsible sources
FSC™ C007454

This book is produced from independently certified FSC™ paper to ensure responsible forest management.

For more information visit: **www.harpercollins.co.uk/green**

Download the audio for this book and a reading guide for parents and teachers at www.collins.co.uk/839709